Be Sweet!

Pam Alexander

Yumion's Mountain Holidays

Third in the Georgia series

Written by: Rhonda Frost Petty
Illustrated by: Pam Alexander

The phrase "Be Sweet" is hidden in the illustrations 7 times in this book.
If you can find them all, you are a true "sweetie."

We would like to dedicate this book

to all our "sweet" models

and to all the people who love Georgia

as much as we do.

RFP and PA

Published by Be Sweet Publications.

ISBN 0-9709105-2-5

Website: www.besweetpublications.com

Yumion's last journey ended in the capitol of gold,
where another adventure was about to unfold . . .

Now he wanted to meet the past U. S. President,
he asked where to find this important state resident!

They told him about The Carter Center;
a great place to visit in summer and winter.

As luck would have it Jimmy Carter was there,
so Yumion asked if he had a few moments to spare.
"Allow me to introduce myself, I'm Yumion.
I'm from Vidalia, home of the sweet onion."

The President said, "It's lovely to meet you,
I'm sure my family would love to greet you.
My hometown of Plains is a lovely place to see,
would you like to share Thanksgiving dinner with me?"

Yumion accepted and they were on their way,
and he was proud to hear the President say,
"It's as ambassadors we are both often viewed,
me for world peace and you for good food!"

Welcome to
Plains
home of
the 39th President

From big city buildings to low rolling lands,
they traveled to Plains and sat down to join hands.
At the Thanksgiving feast prepared with great love,
they all bowed their heads, returning thanks to above:

"Thank you God for all with which we've been blessed:
the food that we eat and the places we rest.
Health, friends, and peace are among the gifts that you've given,
we are thankful for these blessings and others, Amen."

Yumion left to look for a new trail to forge;
after a short trip he ended up at a gorge.
Providence Canyon was this place's real name,
but "The Little Grand Canyon" is its claim to fame.

In the Chattahoochee River, not too far away
was a nice houseboat, what a fine lucky day!
He talked to the captain about getting a ride,
"Of course!" said the nice man, "jump right up inside!"

As the houseboat sailed up near Lake Sidney Lanier,
Yumion said, "I've always wanted to come here.
This Georgia lake has a beautiful view,
I can even see the mountains here too!"

"The Summer Olympics were here awhile back.
The best athletes came here to race their kayaks!"
He stood there awhile, looking back and then forth
kids playing there told him of a town farther north.

He learned more about this small mountain spot
when he stopped to look at a Christmas tree lot.
"In Dahlonega" they said, "There are many gold mines.
If you're lucky, you may find a nugget that shines!"

He was in luck, a new tour was starting.
The guide said, "In a moment we will be departing.
The mine's a bit cool, some of the paths a bit steep,
and bats like it here, but right now they're asleep."

With a lantern lighting the way down the cave,
Yumion wasn't really sure how to behave.
This was a neat place and a nice tour group,
but his stems were so tall that he needed to stoop!

His stems still brushed the roof and caused bats to scatter.
People ducked and looked to see what was the matter.
They saw a scared onion running quickly away,
and shouted, "Come back Yumion! You'll be okay!"

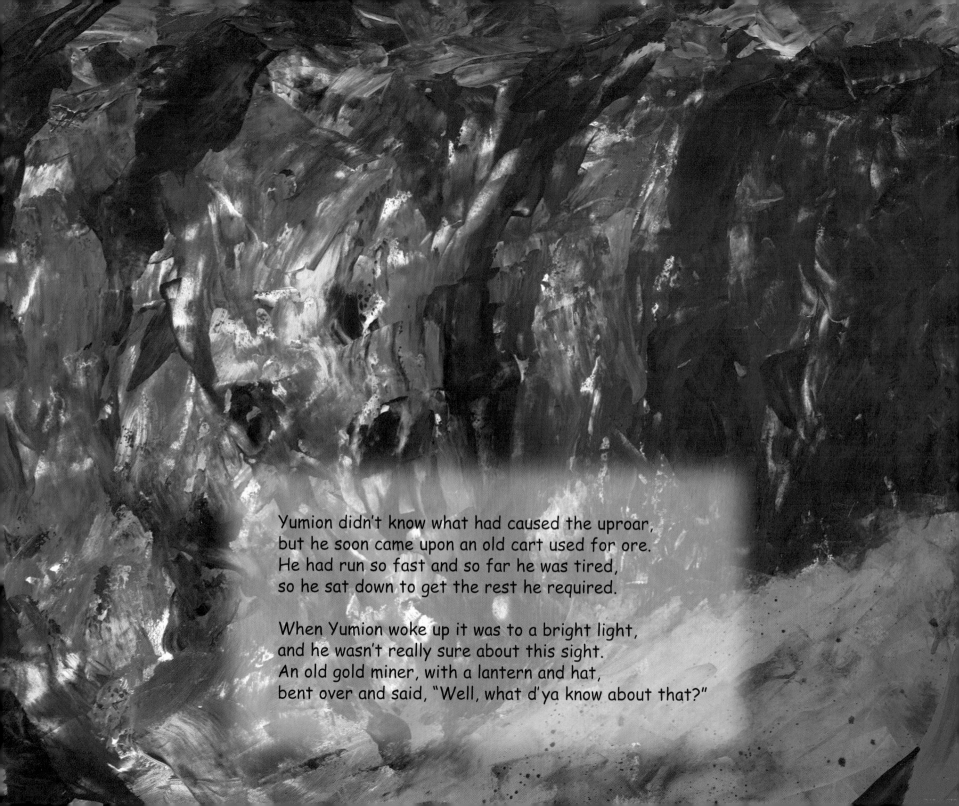

Yumion didn't know what had caused the uproar,
but he soon came upon an old cart used for ore.
He had run so fast and so far he was tired,
so he sat down to get the rest he required.

When Yumion woke up it was to a bright light,
and he wasn't really sure about this sight.
An old gold miner, with a lantern and hat,
bent over and said, "Well, what d'ya know about that?"

Yumion said, "Please help me sir, I'm a very lost onion.
I'm the onion ambassador and my name is Yumion!"
"Nice to meet you Yumion, now let's not be delayed.
If we hurry we can still get to the Christmas Parade!"

The decorations were a spectacular scene;
the town was adorned with bright gold, red and green.
He loved being a part of the grand celebrations,
and Yumion learned of a trail through the huge
Appalachians!

"This trail sounds like a fun time of thrills!"
Yumion said as he started towards the big hills.
His trip up would be long and the way would be steep,
but maybe he'd find a good place to sleep.

He had been hiking awhile when it started snowing.
He was getting quite tired so his pace was now slowing.
There was a bear near the trail eating ripe berries,
this might give Yumion a case of the scaries!

The bear didn't see Yumion standing right there,
and neither did Yumion see the big bear!
They ran down the trail in opposite ways
more frightened than they'd been in all of their days!

During the day, Yumion was a little bolder,
but now it was darker and the snow made it colder.
He looked for some signs on the trees but saw none,
being lost in the woods was not any fun!

When Yumion thought that all hope was gone,
he was just about to mumble and groan.
But then he was sure it was music he heard,
"Could it be?" he thought, and his hopefulness stirred.

He followed the music until he knew he had found it;
a warm little cabin with a porch all around it.
When he looked in he saw some of his favorite things:
a Christmas tree, a family, and a banjo with strings.

He stood there a moment before he was sighted
by two small children who were truly delighted.
They ran to the door and opened it wide,
"Aren't you freezing?" they asked as they brought him insid

Then he noticed the presents under the tree,
"Oh no!" he thought sadly, "I've brought no gifts from me!"
His overall buttons he decided to wrap.
"I don't really need them; I'll just tie up each strap!"

Yumion couldn't believe all the things he could see,
like kids hanging stockings and a beautiful tree.
He saw the joy showing on each person's face,
and thought, "I'm so lucky to be in this place!"

The next morning they found presents from Yumion,
and were touched by the very generous onion.
Another gift was spotted sitting under the tree,
"To Yumion from Santa!" they shouted with glee.

To: Yumion
From: Santa

An overjoyed Yumion opened the present from Santa.
The tag said, "I'm glad you made it here from Atlanta.
Your kindness has made you one who's adored,
so a new pair of overalls is your reward."

So that they could all see, Yumion held them up proudly,
and so they could all hear he proclaimed very loudly:
"I'm an onion ambassador from my stems to my feet,
But ALL Georgia folks make it fun to BE SWEET!"

Important People, Places and Events in this book

President James Earl "Jimmy" Carter, Jr. (left)
Married to Rosalyn Smith Carter, July 7, 1946
Governor of Georgia, 1970-1974
President of the United States, 1977-1981
Founded the Carter Center in Atlanta to promote peace and human rights worldwide.
Won 2002 Noble Peace Prize for his humanitarian efforts.
Has done extensive volunteer work with Habitat for Humanity.

Providence Canyon State Park, also known
as the "Little Grand Canyon" (left)

State Fish - The Large Mouth Bass (Right)

Brasstown Bald, highest mountain in Georgia at 4,784 feet above sea level. (left)

The Appalachian Trail is a continuous marked footpath that goes from Georgia
to Maine for about 2,160 miles. (left)

The first major Gold Rush in America was in Dahlonega, Georgia in 1828.
(left bottom)

Vidalia Onion® Pie

1 1/2 cups chopped and sautéed Vidalia onions® in 1 Tbs. butter

1 Baked 9" deep dish pie shell

1/2 cup pimiento cheese
1 sliced tomato
Cracker crumbs
Parmesan cheese

Preheat oven to 350°. Layer in baked pie shell the sautéed onions, pimento cheese and tomato. Top with cracker crumbs and Parmesan cheese. Bake for 45 minutes.

Lachele Yancey
Winner
Vidalia Onion® Cookoff

If you would like to know if you correctly found all the "Be Sweets" hidden in this book,
go to: www.besweetpublications.com.
However, if you didn't find them all, you aren't a true sweetie, but you are a real good sprout.